MY FEELINGS

Written by Marcia K. Morgan

Illustrated by Christie Sutton Hilty

For additional copies and information concerning speakers and seminars, contact:
Equal Justice
Consultants & Educational Products
P.O. Box 5582
Eugene, Oregon 97405
(503) 343-6761

Library of Congress - TX 1-361-947
First Printing, April 1984
Seventh Printing with revisions, May 1990

Printed in Hong Kong

Dear Parent and Other Caring Adults,

Sexual abuse is not an easy thing to talk about. It has long been a topic filled with fear, secrecy and taboos. Yet like all difficult topics, it is easier to discuss once we begin.

Many parents are reluctant to talk about sexual abuse because it might frighten their children. They believe that somehow, the less information the child receives, the better. We give fire prevention information to our children because we want them to be safe and know how to respond in case of an emergency. Sexual abuse prevention is no different. It is a *safety* issue like learning how to cross the street or not playing with matches.

If sexual abuse prevention is viewed this way, children will receive good, common sense information in a matter-of-fact fashion. They will be more knowledgeable, confident and capable of handling an awkward touching situation. Information does not frighten children. However, confusion and lack of correct information can cause fear. Your child may be more vulnerable than he or she needs to be.

This coloring book is designed to teach children how *effectively* to use their common sense, intuition or *feelings* if confronted with an uncomfortable, confusing or scary touching problem. Children's hunches about OK and NOT OK touches are usually correct and are based on a deep down inner feeling. They need to learn that if they have a NOT OK feeling, it is all right to say "No!" to the person touching them, leave and tell an adult. You can encourage them to trust their own feelings and give them the confidence to respond assertively.

In the back of the coloring book, you will find supplemental information. As you read the coloring book, out loud together, add the information suitable to your child's comprehension and maturity. Discussing the story of Sue and Bart helps establish a healthy, trusting interaction between parent and child. This is important so that your child will feel comfortable in coming to you if he or she has a touching problem.

Sexual abuse is a serious problem that is less likely to occur if we educate our children to recognize the difference between affection and abuse.

Sincerely,

Marcia K. Morgan

Marcia K. Morgan

THIS BOOK BELONGS TO:

NAME _____

STREET _____

CITY _____

STATE _____

TELEPHONE _____

DISCOVER HOW TO BE
SAFE AND SMART
WHEN YOU TRUST YOUR *FEELINGS*
LIKE SUE AND BART.

3

IF SOMETHING'S WRONG
AND CONFUSING TOO,
THEIR **FEELINGS** TELL THEM
WHAT TO DO.

YOU TOO HAVE **FEELINGS**
LIKE BART AND SUE.
FEELINGS ARE LIKE A LITTLE BIRD
WATCHING OVER YOU.

5

IF THERE IS A FIRE
AND YOU SMELL SMOKE,
YOUR *FEELINGS* SAY "LEAVE,
BEFORE YOU CHOKE."

IF A DOG SHOWS HIS TEETH
AND GROWLS REAL LOW
YOUR **FEELINGS** TELL YOU
IT'S TIME TO GO.

YOUR *FEELINGS* TELL YOU
ABOUT TOUCHING TOO.
WHAT'S *OK* OR *NOT OK*
AND THEN WHAT TO DO.

WHEN SOME PEOPLE TOUCH YOU
YOU KNOW IT'S *OK*.
YOU *FEEL* GOOD ABOUT IT
AND SO YOU STAY.

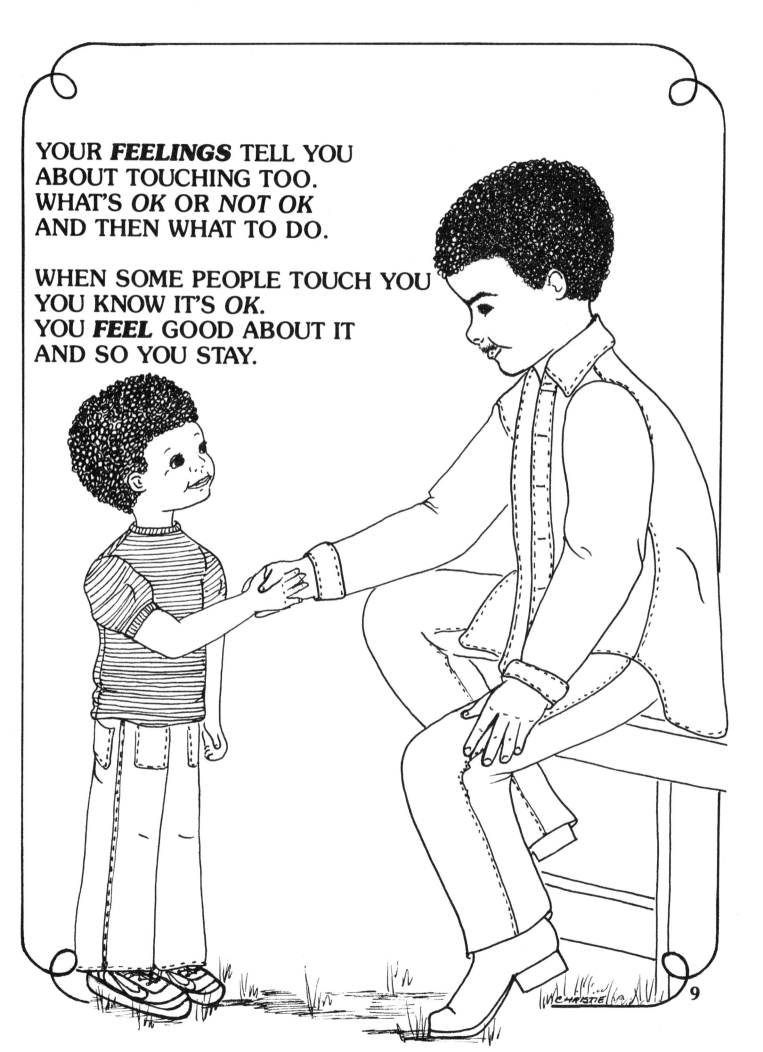

9

IN *OK* TOUCHING
YOU *BOTH* WANT TO TOUCH.
LIKE WHEN *BOTH* PEOPLE WANT
TO HOLD HANDS VERY MUCH....

OR *BOTH* PEOPLE WANT
TO HUG AND TO CUDDLE. . . .

OR *EVERYBODY* WANTS TO FORM A HUDDLE.

SOME TOUCHING IS *NOT OK.*
SOME TOUCHING *FEELS* BAD.
IT MAKES YOU *FEEL* HURT,
SCARED, CONFUSED OR SAD.

IT'S ANYTIME YOU'RE TOUCHED
IN A WAY YOU DON'T LIKE.
YOUR *FEELINGS* TELL YOU
THAT SOMETHING'S NOT RIGHT.

NOT OK TOUCHING COULD BE
A PUNCH IN YOUR STOMACH...

OR A STOMP ON YOUR TOES...

BEING TOUCHED TOO MUCH...

OR TOUCHED UNDER YOUR CLOTHES.

(SOMETIMES YOU JUST DO NOT WANT TO BE TOUCHED AND THAT **FEELING** IS IMPORTANT. YOUR BODY BELONGS TO YOU!)

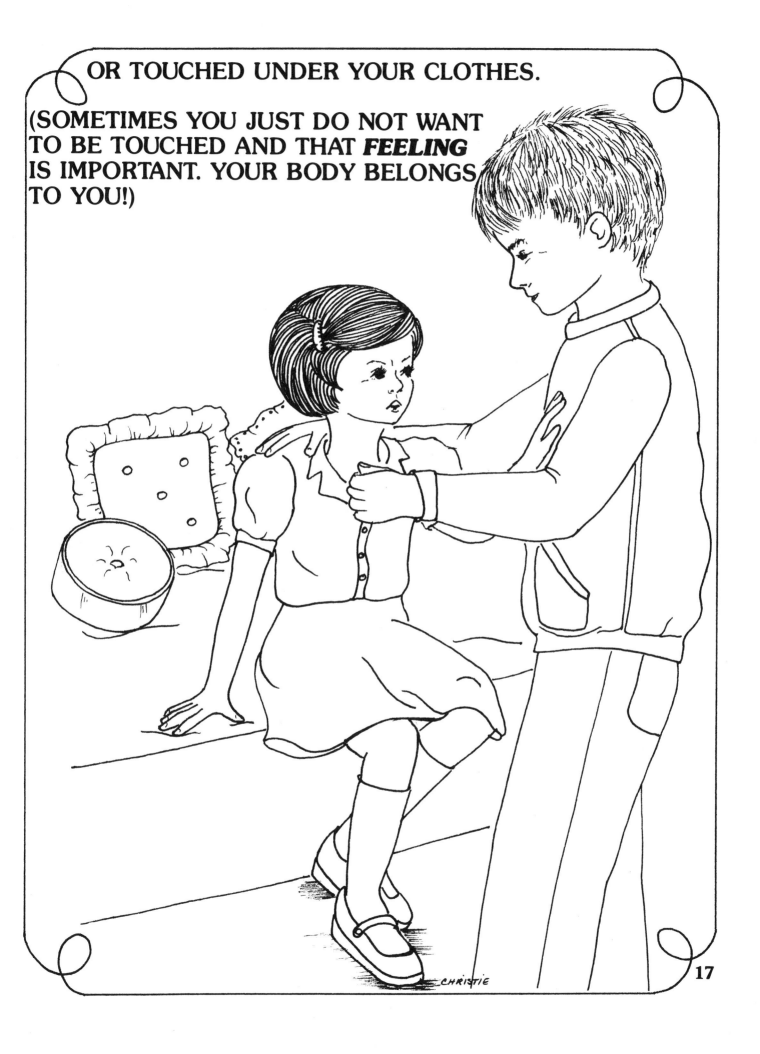

SUE AND BART HAVE BEEN TOUCHED
IN A *NOT OK* WAY.
HERE'S HOW THEIR **FEELINGS**
HELPED THEM OUT ONE DAY.

LEE OFTEN CAME TO SEE
SUE'S MOM AND DAD.
LEE'S ONE OF THE FAMILY
AND SO SHE WAS GLAD.

HE'D ALSO MAKE HER TOUCH HIM
WHEN THEY WERE ALONE, SAYING,
"LET'S KEEP THIS A SECRET,
ALL OF OUR OWN."

SUE KNEW SHE WAS NOT
TO KEEP A SECRET LIKE THIS.
SO WHEN HE TRIED
TO TOUCH AND TO KISS,

SUE'S *FEELINGS* TOLD HER
THAT SHE SHOULD TELL LEE,
"STOP IT!
MY BODY BELONGS TO ME!"

22

SUE TOLD HER MOM
WHAT HAPPENED THAT DAY
AND THAT SHE'D BEEN TOUCHED
IN A *NOT OK* WAY.

HER MOM WAS SURPRISED
WHEN SHE WAS FIRST TOLD.
BUT SOON WAS GLAD
THAT SUE HAD BEEN BOLD.

BART AND HIS FRIENDS LIKE TO MEET AND PLAY NEAR MR. COLLINS' HOME AFTER SCHOOL EVERY DAY.

MR. COLLINS OFTEN
HAD THEM IN FOR ICE CREAM.
THEY ALL HAD FUN
OR SO IT WOULD SEEM.

25

ONE DAY MR. COLLINS
BEGAN TO ACT STRANGE.
ALL OF A SUDDEN
HE JUST SEEMED TO CHANGE.

HE TRIED TO TOUCH BART
UNDER HIS JEANS.
BART *FELT* CONFUSED,
"WHAT DID IT MEAN?"

(THE TOUCHING WAS *NOT OK*)

NOT OK
TOUCHING

"AFTER ALL," THOUGHT BART,
"I NEED TO OBEY.
HE IS AN ADULT.
WHAT CAN I SAY?"

BUT BART'S *FEELINGS* SAID,
"SPEAK UP AND SAY NO.
YOUR BODY IS YOUR OWN.
JUST TELL HIM AND GO!"

CHRISTIE

BART TOLD HIS TEACHER
THE NEXT DAY AT SCHOOL
THAT MR. COLLINS
HAD BROKEN A RULE.

THE TEACHER WAS GLAD
BART DECIDED TO TELL.
MR. COLLINS NEEDED HELP.
HE WAS NOT WELL.

28

AND TELL A GROWN-UP
THEY TRUST VERY MUCH.
ADULTS NEED TO HEAR
ABOUT *NOT OK* TOUCH.

(WHICH ADULT COULD YOU TELL
ABOUT A TOUCHING PROBLEM?)

RELATIVE

FAMILY FRIEND

TEACHER

DOCTOR

COACH

POLICE OFFICER

30

CHRISTIE

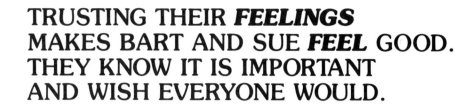

TRUSTING THEIR *FEELINGS*
MAKES BART AND SUE *FEEL* GOOD.
THEY KNOW IT IS IMPORTANT
AND WISH EVERYONE WOULD.

REMEMBER THE LITTLE BIRD
THAT WATCHES OVER YOU.
TRUST YOUR *FEELINGS*
AND BE SAFE TOO!

31

SAD

SCARED

HAPPY

GLAD

ICKY

STRANGE

JOY

CONFUSED

CAUTIOUS

FEAR

ANGER

PLEASED

HURT

MAD

COMFORTABLE

COLOR *OK TOUCH FEELINGS* GREEN
COLOR *NOT OK TOUCH FEELINGS* RED

INFORMATION
FOR
ADULTS

FACTS ABOUT CHILD SEXUAL ABUSE

- 80% of all children who are sexually abused are abused by someone they know or are related to... *not a stranger.*

- 1 in 4 girls and 1 in 8 boys will be a victim of sexual abuse by the time they reach 18 years old.

- Child sexual abuse is any contact with or without force between an adult and child, including rape, sodomy, incest, fondling, molestation and exhibitionism.

- Most children are coerced into the sexual act by bribes, psychological manipulation or trickery. Rarely are they physically forced.

- The average age of a sexually abused child is 8 years old, although it is not uncommon for abuse to begin at a much earlier age. The abuser may be any age, although it is most commonly a male adult or teenager.

- Sexual abuse is likely to occur repeatedly over a period of time with someone the child knows. An incident with a stranger is more likely to involve force and occur only once.

- Children generally do not tell anyone about the abuse because they are frightened and told not to tell by the offender.

- Children often want to tell someone about the abuse but are afraid they will get into trouble, will not be believed nor protected.

- Rarely does a child make-up a story about sexual abuse — each situation should be treated seriously.

- Sexual abuse generally occurs in either the victim's or the offender's home.

- Sexual abuse can happen to any child regardless of social, economic or ethnic group.

Sexual abuse may eventually involve intercourse, but it typically begins with touching...

IMPORTANT POINTS TO TELL YOUR CHILD

1. Say "No!" (to unwanted touch)
2. Leave
3. Tell An Adult

- "Your body belongs to you."
- "You are a very special person and deserve only good, OK touching."
- "You have permission to say no or stop to anyone who bothers, scares or touches you in a way you do not like...even if it is a family member, friend, stranger or any grown-up. People who care about you and your feelings will understand."
- "You may like a person but do not like the way he or she touches you."
- "You do not have to mind adults if they ask you to do something you know is wrong."
- "If anyone touches your breasts, vagina, bottom (for girls) or your penis, testicles, bottom (for boys), come tell me."
- "If someone wants you to touch his/her breasts, penis, testicles, vagina or bottom, come tell me."
- "Did you know it is against the law (or the "rules") for adults and children to touch each other on those parts of the body? It is OK if two adults touch each other there, if both adults want to, but not an adult and a child."

- "You may want to touch and explore your little friends' bodies (i.e. playing doctor). It is normal to be curious and see how bodies are different. But it is Not OK to touch each other's genitals until you are older."

34

- "If anyone threatens you, tries to bribe you (gives you something so you won't tell) or simply makes you feel uncomfortable, say no and leave."

- "Do not keep a secret about touching with an adult or any secret that makes you confused or feel bad."

- "It may be confusing when a doctor touches certain parts of your body (penis, vagina, bottom) or in a way you do not like. If you *feel* that way, tell the doctor and I will come be with you during the exam. If the doctor wants to keep the touching a *secret*, it is Not OK touching." (Other confusing touches such as spanking may need to be discussed. Have the child ask, "Is the touching to be kept a *secret*?" If it is, it is Not OK).

- "If you tell an adult about a touching problem and he or she does not believe you, find another adult to tell. Keep telling until you find someone who does listen and believes you."

- "If you ever have a touching problem with anyone or have any questions, come talk to me about it. I will believe you and protect you. You are not going to get into trouble and you are not to blame for whatever happened."

- "Touching can be warm, caring and nice when both people want to touch. But sometimes it can feel uncomfortable or scary. Not all touching is bad/Not OK nor is all touching good/OK. I want you to know about all types of touching and that you have a right to control who touches your body and who you touch."

IDENTIFYING SYMPTOMS OF SEXUAL ABUSE

Often children will not verbalize what is wrong but will convey the message by a *change* in behavior. The following indicators are helpful in identifying, but may not be isolated to, sexual abuse. Any of these signs could indicate the child is troubled in some way.

Physical Indicators

- Genital or anal injury (swollen, bleeding)
- Venereal disease
- Genital pain and itching
- Change in neatness of appearance
- Gaining weight (wearing loose fitting clothes so as not to draw attention to their body)
- Compulsive masturbation
- Loss of appetite or sudden increase in appetite
- Altered sleep patterns (bedwetting, restlessness, nightmares, fear of sleeping alone, needing a nightlight)
- Newly acquired bodily complaints, especially stomach aches

Behavior and Attitude Indicators

- Extreme shifts of emotion/moods
- Fears and phobias especially aimed at one person or location (if a child is afraid to be alone with someone, such as a relative or babysitter, find out why)
- Suddenly turning against someone, such as one parent
- Restless
- Acting adultlike, inconsistent with age
- Acting childlike (clinging to adult, sucking thumb)
- Frequent absences from school
- Daydreaming - learning problems (drop in grades)
- Irritable, short-tempered
- May ask questions or know terminology inappropriate for child's age
- Expresses affection to adults in inappropriate ways (fondling genitals, french kissing)
- Will not undress for P.E. at school (self conscious of body)
- Hostile and aggressive towards adults or overly trying to please adults
- Afraid to be alone with adult, especially a male
- Isolation (avoids eye contact, withdrawn)
- Shies away from being touched
- Low self-esteem and self-image
- Excessive curiosity about sexual matters (with people and animals)
- Precocious sexual play

35

EDUCATIONAL ACTIVITIES

Pretend Games — Create new situations around the topic of safety. Have children act out their response for each situation. For example, practice answering the door and telephone; what would you do if you needed help walking home from school; what would you do if a relative or a teacher touched you too much; or a neighbor wanted you to touch him/her in a way you did not like; or a babysitter wanted you to undress in front of him/her and then wanted you to touch his/her bottom (penis, vagina, etc.)? Children will feel more sure of their own abilities to handle new situations, to trust their *feelings* and to act in their own best interest. Be sure to balance your examples with good, OK touching situations.

Your Body — Using a doll, picture or pointing to your child's body, teach the correct names for the parts of the body. Tell your child that if anyone touches him or her on certain parts of the body (breasts, penis, testicles, vagina, vulva, bottom or buttocks), even if it feels good, he or she should come tell you. Avoid slang or cute names. Continue to reinforce that their body is their own and no one has a right to touch them *anywhere* on their body if they do not like it.

Feelings — Make five columns on a piece of paper. At the top of each column, list the 5 senses: smell, taste, see, hear and touch. On the left, write the words "OK" and further below that "Not OK." Have children list in each column things they like (OK) and things they don't like (Not OK). For example, I like to taste candy. I don't like to taste spinach. When children get to the touch column, discuss how to recognize OK touches (happiness, caring, both people feel good) and Not OK touches (pain, sweaty palms, tight stomach, confused, scared). All 5 senses feed information to our inner voice and give us an overall *feeling* about people and our environment. Discuss how these *feelings* help us make decisions.

IF YOU SUSPECT YOUR CHILD HAS BEEN SEXUALLY ABUSED...

* Believe what your child tells you
* Tell your child you are glad he/she told you about the abuse
* Do not get angry at your child; stay calm, re-assuring and non-judgmental
* Tell your child he/she is not responsible for the abuse, regardless of the circumstances
* Tell your child you will protect him/her from further abuse by the offender
* Contact your local child protective services, police and/or crisis center. Assist them in anyway you can. If the incident just occurred, do not have your child clean up, change clothes, use the toilet or bathe, or touch anything the offender might have touched.
* Let your child know you are always there to talk and listen. However, try to maintain the normal routine around the house, including chores and responsibilities. Children need the stability.

SPECIAL THANKS TO THE CONTENT REVIEWERS

Margo Belden — Rape Crisis Network. Eugene, Oregon
Lucy Berliner — Harborview Sexual Assault Center. Seattle, Washington
Virginia Friedemann — Children's Services Division. Eugene, Oregon
Shana Denise Hormann — Victim Counselor. Juneau, Alaska
Lynn Landau — Community Advocates. Portland, Oregon
Frances Runkel Lovelace — Teacher. Baker, Oregon
The Rev. Dana Morgan McBrien — Minister. Indianapolis, Indiana
Michael J. Miller — Texas Crime Prevention Institute. San Marcos, Texas
Debra Irwin Moomaw — Englewood Police. Englewood, Colorado
Jack Potter — Former Yolo County School Superintendent. Yolo County, California
John Potter — Criminal Justice Administrator (and my husband). Eugene, Oregon

ABOUT THE ILLUSTRATOR
Christie Sutton Hilty is the mother of two teenage children, wife of a minister, and illustrator. Her life has continually been involved with "the feelings" of others. Christie holds degrees in education and psychology. Her business address is 1905 West 34th Avenue, Eugene, Oregon 97405.

PARENT: CUT AND SAVE

ABOUT THE AUTHOR...

Marcia Morgan, a sexual abuse prevention specialist, lectures throughout the United States and internationally to police, schools and professionals.

Ms. Morgan directed a rape victim assistance program with the Lane County Sheriff's Office in Oregon for seven years and spent three years as a research associate working on a grant from the National Center for the Prevention and Control of Rape, evaluating rape prevention and resistance strategies. She has written and produced two films, *It's OK to Say No* and *Aware and Not Afraid*. She has also authored the curriculum book *SafeTOUCH*, for grades K-5 and co-authored the book *Interviewing Sexual Abuse Victums Using Anatomical Dolls - The Professional Guidebook*.

Marcia and Virginia Friedemann were the original creators of the anatomical dolls now used worldwide in child sexual abuse cases. Their programs have received national attention including being featured on the *Phil Donahue Show* and *Good Morning America*.

Ms. Morgan completed her Bachelors Degree at Oregon State University and her Masters Degree and post graduate work at the University of Oregon.

For information on speakers or setting up a workshop, contact:
Equal Justice, P.O. Box 5582, Eugene, Oregon, U.S.A. 97405 or call (503) 343-6761.

ORDER FORM

Name _____ Organization _____

Mailing Address _____

City _____ State _____ Zip _____ Telephone _____

# OF BOOKS	PRICE PER BOOK	POSTAGE/ HANDLING
1-10	$3.95	$1.25 per book
11-50	3.75	plus 10%
51-100	3.55	plus 5%
101-250	3.35	plus 5%
251-500	3.15	plus 5%
501-1,000	2.77	plus 5%
1,001-5,000	2.40	plus 4%
5,000 +	1.98	plus 3%

Please send me _____ copies of *My Feelings*. Enclosed is my check or purchase order in the amount of $ _____ (US $).

Please make check payable to:
**Equal Justice
Consultants and Educational Products
P.O. Box 5582
Eugene, Oregon USA 97405
(503) 343-6761**

Also available in French.

• •

ORDER FORM

Name _____ Organization _____

Mailing Address _____

City _____ State _____ Zip _____ Telephone _____

# OF BOOKS	PRICE PER BOOK	POSTAGE/ HANDLING
1-10	$3.95	$1.25 per book
11-50	3.75	plus 10%
51-100	3.55	plus 5%
101-250	3.35	plus 5%
251-500	3.15	plus 5%
501-1,000	2.77	plus 5%
1,001-5,000	2.40	plus 4%
5,000 +	1.98	plus 3%

Please send me _____ copies of *My Feelings*. Enclosed is my check or purchase order in the amount of $ _____ (US $).

Please make check payable to:
**Equal Justice
Consultants and Educational Products
P.O. Box 5582
Eugene, Oregon USA 97405
(503) 343-6761**

Also available in French.